Santa's Snow Globe

North Pole

igloobooks

Everyone in the North Pole had finished work for Christmas, except for Santa. Mrs Claus sipped hot cocoa, as the elves sledged down snowy hills. **"Ho-ho-ho!"** called Santa, who was excited to start his deliveries.

Santa carried one last present to the sleigh, as the reindeer munched on crunchy carrots. Suddenly, he tripped and dropped the heavy gift on his big toe. **"Owww!"** cried Santa, clutching his sore foot and hopping around in the snow.

Santa tried everything he could think of to make his toe stop hurting.
First, he put a bag of frozen peas on it. Then, he dipped it in the icy lake.

"Maybe if I put on Mrs Claus' special fluffy slippers," hoped Santa,
"my toe won't hurt so much," but it was no use. It didn't feel any better!

"There's only one thing for it," said Mrs Claus. "We'll have to call the Elf Doctor." Suddenly, he appeared, with a twinkle and a flash. "I'm afraid you must rest your foot tonight," said the Elf Doctor, peering at Santa's big, red toe and shaking his head. "Do not leave the North Pole!"

"Maybe I can go and deliver all the presents, instead," thought Mrs Claus.
So, she jumped into the sleigh and whistled to some of the elves for help.
She pulled on the reins, but to her surprise, the reindeer didn't move!

Meanwhile, Santa called his friend, the magic Christmas Fairy. **"How will the presents be delivered now that I can't do it?"** he asked her.

Just then, the Christmas Fairy appeared with a special gift and said, **"Here, this snow globe is magical. It will help you save Christmas!"**

At that moment, Mrs Claus burst in. "We tried to deliver the presents for you ourselves," she cried, "but the reindeer wouldn't take off!" "Thank you," said Santa, chuckling, "but the reindeer need their magical flying dust." Then, he gave her a special key to unlock the dust store.

Santa began telling them everything they would need to know to do his work for him. **"Here, take these headsets so we can talk to each other,"** said Santa, **"but I'll need to see you to really be able to help."** Then, Santa remembered the magical snow globe. He shook it and saw the sleigh inside.

So, Mrs Claus sprinkled the reindeer with magical dust and they took off into the sky. Sure enough, when Santa shook the snow globe, he saw the sleigh, flying safely above him. **"Where do we go first, Santa?"** asked Mrs Claus, speaking into her headset. He told her the special satnav code and they sped off on their way.

They hadn't gone far, when the reindeer began to feel a bit grumpy! **"Uh-oh,"** said Merry Elf. **"Santa, what should we do?"** Santa spoke over the headset, **"I always keep a secret stash of crunchy apples in the sleigh to cheer them up,"** he said.

Santa watched them in the globe and, before long, began to worry, as it was time for them to land the sleigh for the first time.

Mrs Claus had never driven a sleigh before, let alone landed one on a roof. **"Okay... you'll have to talk me through it,"** she said, feeling nervous.

Santa guided Mrs Claus, step by step, using the magical globe.
"Left a bit, right a bit. Now, pull on the reins!" he called.

With a skid and a bump, Mrs Claus landed the sleigh safely on the roof.
"Ouch!" said Glitter Elf, falling and landing on her bottom.

Inside the house, the elves felt puzzled. **"Which presents do we deliver?"** they asked. Santa looked in the globe and read from his list. Next, he told Sparkle Elf some special magic words so they wouldn't wake the sleeping dog!

Santa helped Mrs Claus and the elves deliver presents all
night long until, soon, they could do it all on their own.
He saw them travel the whole world, inside the snow globe.

In fact, Santa thought they'd all done such a good job of saving Christmas, he wanted to do something special to thank them. With a little help from the Christmas Fairy, he opened the window and called to his North Pole friends.

The Christmas Fairy got straight to work and, with a swish of her magic
wand, the whole of the North Pole was decorated for a special party.
She even made a glittering ice rink for everyone to skate on.
"Perfect," she said, with a twinkling smile.

Jolly Elf helped Freezy Snowman and Fluffy Bunny use the elves' workshop to make some last-minute thank you gifts.

Santa even hobbled to the kitchen and tried to bake some special treats for them, but he burned every last one. **"Oh dear,"** he said.

When Mrs Claus and the elves arrived back at the North Pole,
the snowmen, elves and bunnies all shouted, "**Surprise!**"
Everyone enjoyed the party, whizzing and twirling on the ice, but
Santa was the most excited of all to see Mrs Claus and the elves.